HISTORY OF THE WORLD
in Nine
Guitars

ERIK ORSENNA
accompanied by
THIERRY ARNOULT

translated by
JULIA SHIREK SMITH

HISTORY OF THE WORLD

in Nine

Guitars

WELCOME RAIN PUBLISHERS • NEW YORK

HISTORY OF THE WORLD IN NINE GUITARS
Originally published in France as *Histoire du monde en neuf guitares*
Copyright © 1996 Librairie Arthème Fayard
Translation © 1999 Welcome Rain Publishers LLC.
All rights reserved.
Printed in the United States of America.

Direct any inquiries to Welcome Rain Publishers LLC, 532 Laguardia Place,
Box 473, New York, NY 10012.

Library of Congress Cataloguing-in-Publication Data
Orsenna, Erik, 1947–

    [Histoire du monde en neuf guitares. English]

    History of the world in nine guitars / Erik Orsenna ; accompanied by
Thierry Arnoult ; translated by Julia Shirek Smith.

       p.   cm.

    ISBN 1–56649–046–4

    I. Arnoult, Thierry. II. Smith, Julie Shirek. III. Title.

PQ2675.R7H5713   1999

843' .914—DC21   99–31625

                                     CIP

Book design by Carole McCurdy.
Manufactured in the United States of America by BLAZE I.P.I.

First Edition: July 1999
1 2 3 4 5 6 7 8 9 10

HISTORY OF THE WORLD
in Nine
Guitars

$\mathcal{W}$here?

In the bleak December of a year full of nines,* that cruel little word obsessed the guitar's countless friends: Asian, black, white, and mixed, from all corners of the earth, youngsters with silver rings in their ears and old men in neckties, inhabitants of Rio and Chicago, Berlin and Yokohama, dwelling in elegant urban apartments and the dreariest of public housing.

At the end of the century and the end of the millennium, the gods were tired and tranquilizers no longer

---

* *1999, for those who don't like riddles.*

helped. With bad news so relentless, never had there been such a need for music. When darkness fell, only music could take the anguished by the hand and lead them across the gulf of the night.

Where then? Where would it be held, THE concert, the fabled New Year's Eve celebration?

Friends of the guitar made travel plans, saving up for airfare, offering arms and buttocks for inoculations, drafting excuses to teachers and employers. Fingers walked over maps and globes hour after hour while voices repeated endlessly the same aggressive little syllable: Where?

$\mathcal{T}$he old archaeologist put down the toothbrush and raised his head. He had tried everything: paintbrushes, rags, scrapers. . . . For cleaning the skeletons of our ancestors, however, nothing came close to a good short-handled Butler with soft pig bristles.

Off in the sun an approaching vehicle bounced along, one of those grotesque 4x4s so loved by over-the-hill bleached blondes and all breeds of advertising men. Admittedly, such trucks were useful here, deep in the Africa of sand and ravines. The driver proceeded slowly to avoid running over goats. And perhaps also to absorb through his open window the seductive beauty of the landscape: red plateaus, a bright blue lake dotted with flamingoes, and the fault—suddenly dark and menacing as it seemed to sink into the depths of the earth, down to the Underworld.

The vehicle continued on its course like a ship with sails lowered. It finally came to a halt on the edge of the encampment. For two or three endless minutes the man inside sat motionless, frozen behind the steering wheel. Dust or age had turned him gray. Below the black Ray•Bans the mouth was twisted into a semblance of a grimace or smile.

Finally the door opened. And the old archaeologist immediately understood that the person walking toward him, alone, hand outstretched—in the middle of the desert, hundreds of miles from any town—that this unexpected visitor was first of all a scar. His face looked as if it had been hollowed out by extraordinary rainstorms. As for the salt-and-pepper beard covering his cheeks, apparently it had been grown to keep a little flesh in place. Otherwise, the streams of water would have washed everything away. Life must not have let the fellow off easily.

"Clapton," said the man-scar, removing his sunglasses for a moment. "Am I in the right place? Is this the Omo Valley?"

"It is indeed."

The old archaeologist laid the miraculous toothbrush in its case; he lowered the volume on the CD player, which was playing "Lucy in the Sky with Diamonds"; he offered a chair and tea.

These actions completed, he asked, "And to what do we owe the pleasure of your visit?"

"Music."

The man had a hollow voice, not fully formed. Perhaps he was no longer accustomed to speaking without his guitar, which could be seen in the vehicle, in its place close to him on the front seat.

The old archaeologist smiled. "What can I do for you?" With a slight motion of his chin he indicated the excavation site, a series of holes resembling open graves and filled with workers, black and white. Intrigued by the visit, they had straightened up briefly. They soon resumed their task. Their movements were far too meticulous for gravediggers. Besides, gravediggers do not work with toothbrushes.

The visitor looked and said nothing. Finally he asked, "So, we're in the home of the first humans?"

The old archaeologist swept the air with his right

hand. "You know how experts are: each one believes wholeheartedly in his own theory. . . ."

"I've been told yours isn't far from the truth."

"How can we know?"

But without any prompting, the scientist began his account: "A great forest once covered Africa from the Atlantic to the Indian Ocean. Apes inhabited the region, protected by the trees, by the shade and the tangle of leaves and branches. They moved along on all fours, unhurriedly: no need for caution since their enemies could not see them. Then one day the Earth split open. From north to south, from Ethiopia to Mozambique, a great trough formed, as if Africa were about to divide in two. The floor of the trough filled with lakes; we are on the shores of one of them. There are many others: Victoria, Tanganyika, Malawi, Kivu . . .

"The west wind, which had brought moisture for the trees, now blew against the new mountains born of the fissure. Water no longer came in from the other side. The East was growing drier and drier. The forest thinned out. The apes were alarmed: now it was as bright as day in their territory. Animals with claws—lions and panthers— rejoiced. Henceforth, the apes realized, they would have to be wary and watch for enemies in the distance. They straightened up, stood on their hind legs, learned to fight, to chip stone, and little by little they became human."

Clapton whistled in astonishment. "So it was drought that created us?"

"Correct. Left in the dense jungle, we'd still be apes."

*W*ith one bite the night had devoured the landscape. The diggers had left their tombs almost at a run, as if seized by fear. Now, through the canvas of their tents the flickering of lanterns could be seen. "Lucy in the Sky" played on, lower. Once over, it would start again without a pause.

"You don't like anything but the Beatles?" Clapton asked.

The old archaeologist and his director's chair had disappeared into the darkness. Only the red tip of a cigar indicated where the question was being addressed. "That tune in particular. We had been listening to it steadily back when we discovered our grandmother, fifty-two perfect bones, the first real woman in the history of the world, dating from three million years ago. Now you understand why we named her Lucy."

"And what are you looking for now? An even older skeleton? The mother of the grandmother?"

The old archaeologist remained silent a moment. It was not hard to see that he was rummaging about in the cluttered attic of his hopes and dreams. "Now? . . . I think I would prefer the opposite: the descent down to us . . ." He spoke slowly, as if he had never revealed this desire to anyone and wanted its importance understood. "Now . . . I would dream of welcoming here all of Lucy's descendants, all of them down to us. I wonder how big a crowd that would make . . ."

Clapton could be heard squirming. His denim vest must have been rubbing against the back of the canvas chair.

"What's bothering you?" the old archaeologist asked. "Did I say something I shouldn't have?"

"Lately I've been having the same dream almost every night. My ancestors take me by the hand: a Peruvian peasant, a Catalonian doctor, French king Louis XIV's teacher . . . all of them guitarists, as if by chance. They lead me in a kind of dance. . . ."

"Have you ever had the feeling that all these people are you, different moments of yourself?"

"I don't see what you mean."

"Something tells me you have already lived a number of lives."

"That may be true. The instant I put my fingers on the strings, the second I begin to play, I feel light, as if I'm on a journey. And I'm taken over by characters and eras from the past, unfamiliar words . . ."

"You see! I know little about the guitar, but I suspect it may be some kind of weird horse, a horse that makes it easy for you to travel through the centuries!"

The old archaeologist would have given anything to see his visitor's face at that moment; no doubt it had the look of an astonished child's, in spite of all the scars.

"None of that is very scientific."

"Do you think truth is always scientific?"

For some time the smell of barbecued goat had been drifting through the air, accompanied by the sound of drops of grease sizzling as they fell one by one into the fire. Was it hunger that made the old archaeologist so lively? Or was it the unexpected encounter, which had broken the monotonous routine of the site?

"How far back does the guitar go?" the scientist asked Clapton. "Forgive me, but as you have noticed, I am fascinated by beginnings."

"They've found a guitar on Egyptian hieroglyphics."

"Well, that doesn't make you any younger, does it?"

A shape appeared. In the light of a miner's lamp only the eyes were visible, two white orbs suspended so high in the darkness that it was a question whether they belonged to a human body or to some soaring bird approaching the earth.

"The gentleman will be joining us for dinner?"

The old archaeologist nodded. "The gentleman will be staying with us a few days. If the food is good, perhaps he will play for us what comes after 'Lucy.'"

$\mathcal{A}$nd what do you call this strange instrument?" the pharaoh asked. "I've never seen anything like it. An odd-looking box, extended by an odd-looking handle. And yet I find its precise, subdued notes enchanting."

"*Kitàr,*" replied the musician. "In my country, Persia, *ki* means "three," and for "string" we say *tàr.*"

"I wish it long life, and you as well."

The musician bowed and took his leave. He carried the *kitàr* on his back. The pharaoh's eyes followed him for a long time, until he disappeared over the horizon. Slab by slab, the pyramids slowly climbed toward the sun. A long line of camels was drawing near, laden with great blocks of salt from the other end of the earth. Three pointed sails glided down the River Nile. A fellah lay dozing in the shade of a donkey tormented by flies. In the air, a gentle stirring of objects and living things. The world was new.

The pharaoh sat dreaming awhile, then raised his right hand. A counselor hurried forward.

"Are there many of them, wanderers of this kind?"

"My lord, you may find this disturbing," the counselor replied, "but they proliferate. Today, people can no longer keep quiet nor stay home. They are obsessed with traveling, music slung over their backs."

"But why the need for music? What are they lacking? Drawings, decoration, shapes? That should be enough. Look." The pharaoh pointed to the structures surrounding them, the palaces, the colonnades, the necropoli.

The counselor shrugged. "They say a forest spirit is the cause of this madness."

"The forest? There is nothing but sand here!"

"That's just it, they also say that music is a form of yearning."

$\mathcal{T}$he Incas watched as tears ran down their emperor's cheeks.

They were not mistaken; they had guessed correctly the nature of those tears, which had nothing to do with fear. An emperor, child of the Sun, is afraid of no one. The emperor wept from another cause: the emperor wept from astonishment. He could not understand why 182 strangers had come from afar to tear the world apart.

Before the arrival of the 182—curse them!—all had been calm, with each bit of the universe in place. In the sky above reigned the Sun God; beneath the feet of men the Earth Goddess throbbed with life. The Earth was the mother of all. Her children spoke to her with flutes and drums. She replied with the rumbling of volcanoes, the rustling of forests, and the bubbling of springs. The Earth even grew loquacious at times, when the winds were strong. The ears of corn ripening on their stalks would bounce against each other—*cha-ca, cha-ca*—and people danced to that muffled beat.

Then, why, mounted on their fearsome animals, brandishing hollow sticks filled with fire, had these 182 sailors come to kill the Incas and upset the ancient order of things?

And Emperor Atahualpa wept.

When the country in his charge is rent asunder, an emperor weeps. The tears he sheds are the blood of a wounded world.

Francisco Pizarro, the Spaniard, leader of the 182, dismounted. The emperor did not look at him. The emperor never looked at anyone. The emperor kept his eyes eternally raised toward his father, the Sun.

"Offer him gold," the emperor said to the interpreter, "as much gold as he can take away. That's the only thing these strangers like. Maybe, with their pockets filled and their animals laden, they will leave the sky and the Earth in peace."

The emperor went on weeping. Tears of amazement, tears of incomprehension.

Francisco Pizarro was a sensitive soul. He could not stand those tears. He gave an order. Spurs jangling, three of his henchmen stepped up to the emperor, put their big, dirty hands around his throat and strangled him before the terrified populace.

And now Atahualpa lay dead on the stones of the courtyard.

Nothing seemed different. The water in the river did not flow back to its source. The condors as wide as windmills went on endlessly tracing circles above the mountains.

But the Incas realized that the world was dead and that the reign of curses had begun.

Among the 182 was frail and pale José Fernandez, forever lagging behind, constantly jostled, ridiculed for his timidity, a Spaniard quite unlike his fellow soldiers: he was all gentleness, respect for others, and curiosity about the world. Sickened by the emperor's murder, he had left the little army and set off into the countryside alone. He might have been a traveling merchant. In lieu of a firearm, he lugged around an enormous black case. He was further weighed down with a large bag and countless containers. The duke of Càdiz, mad about exotic plants and remedies, had assigned him the mission of inventorying the botanical riches of the New World. While his comrades were murdering and plundering, José spent his days sketching, botanizing, and filling his pockets with specimens. Unbeknownst to the Catholic Church, the duke had entrusted him with another mission: that of having sexual relations with as many women as possible and describing in detail original practices of the tropics.

That's where the black case came in.

Several times a day, whatever his surroundings, José Fernandez would take out his guitar. At home, in Spain, that action alone used to prompt a rash of song. Birds chirped their heads off, women undid two buttons on their bodices, men spit out their plugs, the wheat in the fields danced. . . . Here in the highlands of curse-stricken Peru, men in red ponchos, women in voluminous skirts, and children with green snot on their faces would all look at him wordlessly. And the Earth kept silent.

No more help from a murmuring wind, no more tunes hummed in the leaves, no more joyful beat in the cornfield. Nothing. The world's silence covered its inhabitants like a heavy gray lid.

And as if a reminder of the damnation, high above the peaks and the snows and the silence circled the condors, wings wider than the sails of the invading fleet.

The guitar had lost its powers. Its notes encountered no echo. They came up against emptiness. Any words the universe could speak had been left in the martyred throat of the Emperor Atahualpa.

*I*n northern Peru, one evening at dusk an armadillo crossed the road. A kind of large porcupine who looked as if he had traded his quills for scales. He moved along at a leisurely pace, in love perhaps or just content to drink in the cool of the evening. Fernandez pointed at him. The Incas understood the message and, dancing up to the animal, bowed to the ground: "A thousand pardons, Sir Armadillo, but the Earth does not answer us, and we must try everything." And they picked him up; his little paws twitched in the air. And all the while asking his forgiveness, they turned him into a guitar. His shell, emptied of its innards, became the sound box; a wooden neck replaced his head; and his intestines, dried, were melodious strings.

Fernandez smiled. His work was done. With their animal guitar to supplement the drums and flutes, the Incas now possessed all of music's resources and could enter into dialogue with the Earth. She would soon stop pouting.

Provided that he, the stranger, departed.

He walked to the sea. He rested on the sand.

What was he waiting for? A Seville-bound ship? Or death?

Sunburned and thirsty, he felt no hunger. He sat and looked at his guitar. It lay on the beach, at the water's edge, like a small vessel ready to set sail.

A feeling of great joy had swept over the musician. He had guessed what was to come: the guitar would produce offspring everywhere, a family infinitely diverse, of the strangest shapes and materials, a family that would soon cover the planet. No shame, no sorrow, no silence would be able to withstand all those guitars. Guitarists were the knights of the tempestuous alliance between the Earth and humanity.

$\mathcal{C}$lapton awakened in the tiny borrowed tent, frozen. Enclosed in his sleeping bag, he poked his head outside. The camp was asleep.

Two bearers, bundled up in long brown cloaks, held their hands over the embers of a dying fire. The musician and the nomads exchanged solemn nods. Animals, invisible in the dark, were chewing slowly. Their breathing and the rhythmic scraping of their jaws could be heard. The moon lent the air a slightly dizzying transparency, a clarity like that in dreams where distances seem non-existent.

"Not surprising," Clapton said to himself, "that I am traveling so effortlessly through time and from one end of the planet to the other. The African night is a vessel without anchor."

And he stretched out again. A concert of gurgles rose from his gut. Grilled goat was not like a cheeseburger: it did not yield to digestion without a fierce struggle.

BARCELONA, 1580

*I*n that blessed June bells rang out, adults knelt to thank God, children frolicked, crickets sang, the sun shone newly bright, the sea sparkled as never before: the plague was at an end.

For ten months the epidemic had consumed everything: newborns and the aged, full-bosomed beauties with luscious lips as well as the ugly and withered. Every resident of Barcelona would awaken terrified, wondering: Is it my turn today? And each body would be self-examined for symptoms—their nature, alas, known only too well—which might have made inroads under the cover of night. Well, am I shaking with fever? There, under the arms, or at the top of the thighs, am I brooding pigeon eggs? Good Lord, I just coughed; better bring the candle over; am I going to find blood in my sputum?

Not satisfied with killing human beings, the epidemic had attacked that Catalonian specialty, enjoyment of life. It had emptied the taverns, where patrons had spent whole nights constructing a world of abundant gold and faithful women. Impossible to clink glasses with someone whose acrid breath could carry disease! The epidemic had driven away the perfumes of the port with all their variety and fascination—from the spices of the East to the basils of Provence, from the animal musks to the scents of the gypsy fortune tellers. People went about with cloths over their noses to escape the stench of death.

The epidemic had prevented strolling. No longer did anyone walk up and down Las Ramblas, that shaded avenue where the folk of Barcelona had formerly met, exchanged insults, and whispered of assignations. Minds were taken over by wild fears, the most notable a dread of catching furuncles from a glance alone.

The epidemic had even murdered that daily wonder, the Barcelona sunset. So many corpses were thrown on so many funeral pyres that a curtain of black smoke kept the horizon in perpetual mourning.

And what can be said about the life led by doctors during this nightmare?

Up before dawn, Doctor Amat ran all over town: from the mount of the Jews, who believed they could escape the scourge by immersing themselves in incomprehensible books, to the house of the canons, where they were trying out a new sulfur lotion; from the Court of the Orange Trees, where lay more than a thousand bedridden, to Saint Eulalie Cathedral, where the nuns implored God to halt the curse.

. . . That time of horror was over. Make way for pleasure! Cool and comfortable in his bedroom, protected from the heat by thick walls and from the harsh light by drawn blinds, his belly full and his thirst quenched, rested after his first real night's sleep in ten months, the doctor now lay stretched out between a young woman and a guitar. He asked himself what order to follow, which pleasure to take first, for those exhausting weeks had deprived him as much of love as of music.

*W*ell, what do you see in her?" the young woman asked, annoyed. She had been waiting for the lovemaking to begin.

"Light on the thigh, gentle against the trousers, blond to the eye, rounded and sweet-smelling in the arms . . ."

"And that's it?"

"Oh, no. She is also unassuming. And modest, never in a hurry to fill the leading role, preferring instead to play in the background, to accompany. She is unacquainted with the sickness of pride consuming the world."

"I see," said the young woman. "The ideal, so to speak!"

"And yet she is proud, knowing better than most how to command respect. Some days, there is nothing to be gotten from her: You know how it is: the sore fingers are in vain; she screeches, hisses like an army of enraged cats. It is her way of protesting: stop right there, my love, you do not know how to treat me, change your ways at once."

"But you're talking about passion!"

"And a homebody, domestic, adores napping on the bed, loves to purr while her wood is caressed by a rag dipped in beeswax. But quivers with pleasure when sensing a trip in the air, ready in a flash to brave the perils of the highway and the dust of the road."

"I don't know what I'm doing here!" The young woman picked up her skirts and fled the scene. Her hands shook, and red blotches had appeared on her neck—with blondes a better proof of genuine distress than tears.

Doctor Amat sighed. Of course, he had been tactless. It is not polite to force on a guest the portrait of her rival. But, the temperament of these Catalonian women! Life was certainly magnanimous enough (and beds wide enough) for threesomes!

A month went by. After a week of exuberance, life had reassumed its usual course and death its old habits. No longer did people pass away from anything other than old age, violence, and too much wine.

The plague was indeed gone. It had been spotted far away, elsewhere, on the south shore of the Mediterranean, around Algiers and Tunis—regions where, in any case, it was best not to venture and risk being taken into slavery.

Now that the infection had moved on, now that the

sky was again pure and the sun blazing, why did the townspeople retain their pestilence-inspired gestures, their condemned-to-death walk (small steps, left hand over the mouth), the sober and frugal habits of the sick (no visits to cabarets, tiny purchases at the market)? Why those despondent looks on the faces in the street? Why the hushed tones, the whispering, why such prudishness in the women, such ennui in the children?

Little by little, the doctor began to suspect he had the answer to all these questions. A depressing answer.

Suppose the plague had not departed alone? Suppose it had taken in its luggage something secret and invaluable, a commodity whose movement no accountant, however meticulous, would have thought of recording in his ledgers, a kind of color and scent, a vibration in the air, a spark, almost a song: the soul of Barcelona, its genius for happiness?

Doctor Amat sent his patients away and locked himself in his office. And Anna Maria, his assistant-nurse-guardian angel-cook-business manager–supplier of local gossip, was spreading a bizarre story around town: "My master has come up in the world. My master isn't a doctor for people any more. Now he has cities under in his care."

For two months he did not go out. Every day Anna Maria left oranges, rice black with cuttlefish ink, and works he had requested from the library at his door. The good servant glued her eye to the keyhole and muttered, "God in heaven, what's happening to my master? Is he angry with the guitar he used to love so much? Has he forgotten how to play? Why the beginner's exercises? Is it his second childhood? The plague has surely destroyed his mind!"

She would go off finally, her wooden shoes scraping against the stone floor, her lips moving in prayer as she asked the Virgin Mary to deliver her master from his madness.

After 150 days and 150 nights of relentless labor, Doctor Joan Amat came out of his office, blinking with fatigue, guitar in the left hand, a sheaf of papers in the right. He almost knocked over Anna Maria, who, as usual, had been spying on the worker and his sounds.

"Thanks be to God," she said on her knees, "you are back among the living!"

The very next day, Joan Amat began practicing medicine again. But he had changed his methods of treatment. To all his patients, along with recommendations for devout and healthful living, he would give a copy of his opuscule, the first guitar book for beginners.

A month later, all traces of the epidemic—the horrible sights, the unforgettable stench—had disappeared as if dissolved by the music. The city had recovered its gaiety of former days. Everywhere the Catalonian air resounded with notes, chords, and refrains. At every intersection, someone played; seated on street markers or behind open windows, people sang; others, even as they strolled along the avenues, managed to strum the strings while picking their noses (a Mediterranean specialty).

A band of children always followed the doctor, for he talked as he walked: "Here is a healthy city. . . . The guitar has saved Barcelona. . . . The guitar is our most powerful friend. . . . On this earth there are three pairings that count: a man and a woman, a man and his horse, a man and his guitar. . . ."

*W*hen age and illness caught up with him and he had to take to his bed, doctors and priests flocked to his side. Not for anything would they have missed the demise of such a famous person. Especially intriguing was the spectacle of his great composure.

The doctor did not want to believe in his approaching death. He no longer had the strength to play, but his hand did not stop stroking the Toledo guitar that lay beside him on the linen coverlet.

"I am not dying," he repeated.

The doctors shook their heads with knowing and superior looks.

"I am not dying."

"Now don't be too optimistic, my dear colleague."

"I am not dying."

"If that's what you say."

"I am not dying."

"As you wish, but that's no reason to insult Science! Nor to offend God!"

The priests had joined the doctors in the bedchamber and, like them, were outraged over the patient's obstinate unwillingness to die. They tried to snatch his guitar away. Wasted energy: he held it very tight. Sensing there was witchcraft about, they called in the inquisitor, who (with the help of torture) had restored more than one hundred heretics of various sorts to the paths of righteousness before burning them. In his presence, Joan Carlos Amat continued the litany: "I am not dying. I shall never die."

"Might you, my son—and this would be most grave— might you be harboring the sacrilegious idea that you are immortal?"

"The guitar is the perfect form. . . . The guitar is the image of the soul. . . . The guitar and guitarists travel through time."

Faced with this blasphemy, the inquisitor crossed himself, horrified, as were all those in the room.

Doctor Amat's voice had grown even weaker. They had to lean over to hear him. Now he was reciting names: "Richard the Lion-Hearted, Guiraut Riquier of Narbonne, Juan of Palenria . . ."

"The king of England I'm familiar with," the inquisitor muttered. "But who are the others?"

"Guitarists, Monsignor," said the choirmaster, a man learned in musical history. "Famous guitarists of their time, sons of God for all that . . ."

Doctor Amat went on: "Alfonso of Toledo, Rodrigo de la Guitarra."

"And who are they?"

"*Idem,* Monsignor, instrumentalists of renown."

Doctor Amat's voice was now only a whisper: "Franceso Corbetta, Fernando Sor, Andrés Segovia, Django Reinhardt, Jimi Hendrix . . ."

"Unknown," stammered the choirmaster (he appeared to be kissing the dying man, so close was his ear to the poor wretch's lips), "those names are completely unknown to me."

"Allies of Satan!" screamed the inquisitor. "Have them sought out at once, and as for him, have him put to the rack at once!"

But it was too late.

With a final contraction of his right hand sounding a seventh chord in the silence of the horrified room, Doctor Joan Carlos Amat, author of the first method for amateurs and savior of Barcelona, had breathed his last.

VERSAILLES (FRANCE), 1680

$\mathcal{W}$elcome, Master . . ."

The carriage had come to a halt in the castle court-yard. After all those days on the road (dusty, bumpy, boring), life had suddenly taken on an air of fairy tale and formality. Soldiers were presenting arms, while a ceremonious trio stood in waiting, hats off and perruques immaculate.

"Master Corbetta, it is an honor to welcome Italy's most famous musician. . . ."

"Master, we understood your fatigue, but His Majesty the king awaits you. . . ."

The master, for master he was, stretched, shook himself, and took a few deep breaths. Picking up his guitar, he stepped onto French soil and followed the trio, whose leader, a ruddy-faced giant, emitted an unending flow of honeyed phrases, like a fountain on a feast day: "Master Corbetta this, Master (simply) that . . . Your knowledge of harmony . . . Your gift for accompaniment . . . Because of you the instrument . . . In musical Europe they talk only of you. . . . His Majesty cannot wait to welcome you. . . ."

A bailiff ahead of them, the little company entered a labyrinth: endless corridors, drawing rooms as vast as cathedrals, corridors again, and always a crush, a dressed-up crowd, marquis and duchesses standing in conversation or sitting at cards, dice, and backgammon. No street, even on market day, had ever seen such congestion.

"Make way, please," whispered the ruddy giant.

Courtiers looked the stranger over with disdain, but upon noticing his guitar, they would immediately bow and step back.

"Could it be . . ."

". . . Master Corbetta, the virtuoso, guest of the king?"

The noble ladies were already making eyes at him; the

men were crafting personable smiles. How could they make friends with the new favorite?

The Italian could not help gasping, "Good Lord, I can't breathe!"

The giant turned around: "Do not be alarmed. Surely it is only travel fatigue. Besides, we are almost there. There is no better medicine than the presence of the king. You shall see how handsome he is."

*I*t is here."

With his chin the giant indicated a massive red door. He seemed timid now, like a child facing the school entrance for the first time. His two acolytes smoothed down their perruques, bit their lips, and danced from one foot to the other in the manner of humans with a pressing need. The giant tried three times: his first two taps on the door were overly discreet and thus inaudible.

"What is it this time?" came a shout from within. "Will we never be left in peace, even in this place?"

"With my deepest respects, sire. Master Corbetta has arrived."

"Finally, God be praised! Have him come in! Why is he late?"

The giant grabbed the Italian by the arm, whispering, "Good luck," followed by, "There is no possibility of error. You will recognize His Majesty straightway; he shines like the sun." He cracked open the red door and with a nudge dispatched the traveler into the Holy of Holies.

A strange gathering.

A circle of ten persons sat enthroned on chairs with wide platforms and high backs. Their attire was elegant: lace, ribbons, embroidery. Only their hose lacked nobility: it had been pulled down over the buckled pumps, revealing hairy white calves.

"Welcome," said one of the seated. "You have been keeping us in suspense."

To be honest, the Italian did not notice any particular majesty about the man who had addressed him so brusquely, although with regard to the great bulbous nose and the rather small dimensions of the rest of his person, the king of France, Louis the Fourteenth by name, did indeed live up to his reputation. The Italian stammered an inaudible litany crammed with "thank you's," "great honor's," "sorry's," "endless journey's," and "rutty road's."

"Do stop talking," said Louis. "Let's get on with it." He grabbed the guitar, which had been resting at the foot of the chair, doglike, as it docilely awaited the royal pleasure.

In spite of his fatigue, the Italian master began the lesson. "First, posture. Spine straight, shoulders relaxed. Right leg to the side. Place the instrument on the left knee and point the neck toward two o'clock."

The monarch followed directions. "Very good," said the master, and the courtiers applauded daintily.

"Now, sire, the technique we call *tirando*. The finger pulls the string in the manner of an archer releasing his arrow."

Louis XIV acquitted himself creditably. The master expressed his pleasure; the infatuated courtiers smiled broadly and renewed their silent applause.

"Now let us go on to *apoyando*."

After two hours of putting the king through his paces, the Italian decided to bring this first session to a close. He was staggering from lack of sleep, his mind filled with images of beds, sheets, pillows, counterpanes. But how to interrupt a monarch whose august (and pudgy) digits took such malicious delight in torturing the strings?

His sojourn with the duke of Mantua had taught Corbetta a courtly trick or two. He placed his guitar on the floor and applauded, soon imitated by the ensemble of seated courtiers.

"Why all the fuss?" inquired Louis XIV, with false modesty.

"Sire, in twenty years of teaching, never have I run across such talent."

"Amazing," added a courtier, shaking his head so forcefully that powder fell from his perruque.

"Dazzling," said his neighbor, going a bit farther.

"Astounding, astonishing, discouraging . . ."

Each one contributed his compliment.

"Do you really think so?" simpered the king. "Should I believe you?"

The Italian took advantage of the situation: "Sire, with such application and such a natural gift, in six months the pupil will have surpassed the teacher."

"Maybe less," ventured one courtier in a whisper.

"Five."

"Four and a half!"

Before another courtier could offer a bid, the Italian master raised his hand and released a volley of proverbs: "Rome wasn't built in a day." "Let well enough alone." "Grasp all, lose all. . . ."

"I get it," said Louis XIV, and he deigned to let there be silence.

The Italian felt relieved. The grating, squeaky notes produced by beginners, royal or not, are likely to torture even the most battle-hardened eardrums. And the silence that briefly filled the air seemed the most soothing of melodies.

Then why did the king have to stand up, followed immediately by the ten courtiers?

Up to that moment the air had not smelled of roses, and occasional whiffs of nauseating effluvia had assailed the nostrils; fortunately the forest of hairs in those regions provided something of a filter. But, intent on his teaching and intimidated by the august character of his pupil, Francesco Corbetta had paid scant attention to the olfactory unpleasantness. French palaces are like that, he told himself: a feast for the eye but an ordeal for the nose. I shall have to get used to it. One cannot have everything, and so on.

That stoic wisdom, that impassivity proved no match for the new and terrible attack of which his nose was soon the victim. A wave of pestilence overwhelmed the room. Having a native curiosity about causes, Francesco sought the reason for the horrible smell. The inquiry did not take long.

An observation worthy of note: no one will ever claim that Italy is a stranger to the commode, among the most practical of toilet facilities. Moreover, the peninsula is conversant with the rank and the rotten—one need only visit Naples on a torrid August day! But although we may engage in every sort of gastronomic and amorous activity in our opera boxes, to my knowledge we have never yet mixed music and defecation.

Francisco Corbetta thought he had already seen all there was to see on this, his first day at Versailles.

No sirree!

To his surprise, no sooner had the noble lords stood up than they pulled from their pockets large batiste handkerchiefs edged with lace.

Good Lord, the Italian said to himself, they are going

to blow their noses! My music has given them colds. Or else long hours of exposure on those chairs has chilled them from within.

He was wrong.

In unison, they leaned over and—I am ashamed to say it, because the French court was known all over Europe for its unparalleled refinement—they wiped themselves, slowly and carefully, never ceasing to smile lovingly at the king. His Majesty, while busy with the same intimate task, was uttering impressions and issuing orders: "We are quite happy with your services, Master Corbetta. We think a year of practice will bring us up to your level. So we say to you: tomorrow, same time, same place."

And Louis XIV left the room, followed single file by his sycophants, who one by one tossed their dirty linen into the blue porcelain vase proffered by a valet with pinched nostrils.

MILAN, 1820

*P*arma, in northern Italy, country of the world's loveliest lakes. The air carries a hint of the south and the sun. Chestnut trees dominate the countryside, but in family courtyards it is orange trees that are everywhere. Here gardens move: the giant red earthenware pots must be brought indoors before winter.

Parma.

In the October mist the day dawned tentatively. A tall, slender silhouette, hunched over and a bit crooked, could be seen passing by Santa Cecilia Maggiore. At the corner of the church, the figure turned and cut across the empty square, then headed toward the Campo Farnese.

Bareheaded, longish hair dripping wet, greatcoat with upturned collar, a long black box under his arm, the man hugged the walls and disappeared into the fog.

One bell, then two, had just rung in the campanile. Six o'clock?

Later, not far away, Via Giulia, another apparition, this one departing a house and carefully shutting the door. The hinges squeaked a little. The figure turned—a glance to the right, a glance to the left—and at a leisurely pace, with the relaxed step of the satisfied lover, a black case in each hand, stumbling on the glistening cobblestones, he too faded into the opaque air.

A duel in the pale light of dawn?

Some nasty business dragging on since summer?

*F*or whom are we waiting?"

"Paganini, the illustrious Nicolo Paganini."

The coachman was swaggering. The passenger felt like cursing. The Parma-Milan mail coach had already been delayed half an hour. But the coachman was beaming. He would be able to recount the event for months: "I'm telling you, I have transported Paganini!"

"Easy, easy!" He quieted his horses the best he could.

Inside the coach, Luigi Legnani was raging and grumbling: "Paganini . . . I was sure of it! A violinist. And of the worst sort. The Great Whore."

He cursed, he swore. Once again, he berated himself. He called himself an idiot. If he had it to do over, he too would have chosen the violin rather than the damned guitar! As long as he had to practice scales and arpeggios six hours a day . . . The present age liked nothing but the violin, its sobs, its billing and cooing. And women were interested only in violinists. Hadn't Chiara said to him the other night, "My poor love, why play an instrument nobody hears?" Women nowadays loved the din of the heart, noisy sentiments. That's why they swooned before the violin. They had become too lazy to strain their ears.

One thing was certain: if he had preferred the violin, it was he who would now be late, delayed by some bit of good fortune, instead of waiting, a wretched guitarist champing at the bit, crammed between a peasant smelling of strong cheese and a fortyish lawyer type with a potbelly.

The coachman began to worry. The sun was up. The passengers were heard from. The coach should be leaving!

Too bad for Paganini. That evening's concert would be canceled. The next morning the Milanese would fight even harder to hear the wonderful-if absentminded-unbearable-charming-virtuoso-latecomer.

Just then two black cases flew into the baggage carrier. And a large shape tumbled to the ground, tie crooked, hair unkempt, laugh thunderous, far too loud for the early hour . . .

"Lost my footing! I slipped on the footboard. My apologies, everyone."

"Don't mention it, master."

"You didn't hurt yourself, did you?"

They forgave him, they crowded around him. The rude fellow found the homage natural. He dusted himself off and caught his breath.

"Well, what do you know, it's good old Luigi! Ladies and gentlemen, let me introduce a genius of the guitar. It's been a long time! You're doing well? What luck! Come on, crack the whip, coachman! Make up for my shocking lateness!"

*I*l *Cannone! Il Cannone!"*

Naught to do with those little springtime successes so loved by the citizens of Parma: shaking the pharmacist's plump hand, brushing up against the magistrate's daughter, kissing monsignor's ring.

"Il Cannone! Il Cannone!"

The first time the shouts had rung out, the able-bodied men of Parma rushed to take up their positions. What positions? Parma had never been known for its military spirit.

"Il Cannone! Il Cannone!"

The rumbling always came from the ticket windows and the doors of the theater. Chanted for hours before opening time.

The men would fight; women would cry out and fall to the pavement as if dead, white-faced and stiff. For a place near the stage, people would break down doors, crawl under seats, and kill one another. Shame on Parma!

And on everywhere else, for that matter: over each hill would come long lines of stagecoaches, cabriolets, and elegant tilburies. Enthusiasts of all sorts, severe Paris critics and painted showgirls, arriving from the ends of the earth for the performance, sometimes from as far as Boston.

Il Cannone: world famous.

Buckets of cold water would go from hand to hand—sleeves rolled up, manly laughter—to be poured in a steady stream over a crowd gone mad. To no avail.

Il Cannone!

"The Cannon," as they called it, was his violin. Paganini's violin. A Giuseppe Guarneri del Gesù with a short neck (Cremona, 1742). Preferred to the Stradivarius for the resonance and power of its body.

Wherever Nicolo had gone in the last three years, the public tracked down his carriage and found his hideaway. To touch Paganini, to make off with his cravat or a lock of hair . . .

"The master of the violin" was the journalists' stock phrase. And he would add with a snicker, "But the guitar is my master."

That would be taken as something of a pose.

Poor guitar! The instrument not heard.

*F*or at least two hours they had been bouncing in the ruts as they drove by a third lake, which seemed to go on forever. A flask—of rather dubious Madeira—made the rounds. That was the custom: one wine per lake, a Piedmontese invention for killing the boredom of the road.

And Luigi kept his eyes on Paganini, his friend of childhood days. Paganini had not stopped smiling at him. Paganini was playing amiably. Violinist style, to be sure: vulgar, loud, the style of the fawned-upon star. But those efforts were notorious. And touching. Paganini wanted to renew their connection. But what connection? Friendship is not a piece of heavy twine; what it has tied together comes apart. What keeps a friendship going? It will last until death, the friends think. And then life, petty jealousies, hidden hurts, gradually pull them apart. They drift away from each other like two ships at sea. Imperceptibly at first, reluctantly. Then each one makes his own wake and disappears into a corner of the horizon.

Luigi looked at the violinist's huge hands, the oversized digits which had made the family doctor so uneasy: "An exceedingly long, scrawny infant; abnormal limbs, precursors of degeneration and probably epilepsy."

And now those very fingers were racing across sheets of staff paper, in spite of the jolts and fearful shaking which threatened to destroy the vehicle at any moment.

Huddled up, bent over, teeth rattling, Paganini was composing in his notebook. He composed furiously, all the while smiling at Luigi. Violinists and their pretty-boy clown ways might be detestable, but what vitality this one had!

The passengers, despite the Madeira and the long ride, were silent. Fascinated, they sat staring at the master and his antics; they nudged each other. In a few years they would look back at this enchanted moment: "Yes, we traveled on the same coach. Yes, we saw Him create. We witnessed the birth of a masterpiece."

"Whew," said Paganini as they rode into Milan. "No easy task. But here it is. A brand new sonata in A major. For violin and guitar . . ."

And he extended the wrinkled notebook to Luigi. "Something to reconcile you with music. As much for the guitar as for the violin . . ."

Alerted somehow, a small crowd was waiting impatiently in front of the inn. It immediately surrounded the vehicle.

"Il Cannone . . . Il Cannone!"

"Ah, here we go again," said the master. "As soon as you've warmed up your fingers, come join me. We'll whip it into shape before dinner. And after, glory will be ours! Don't forget: Violin *and* guitar. Glory à deux."

$\mathcal{L}$uigi had chosen a room at the far end of the hallway. A quiet spot, narrow like a case. A room for the guitar. One luxury: the fireplace, in which three logs burned brightly. He had blown out the candles. The light from the flames was adequate for sight-reading the sonata by the "master," the so-called "masterpiece" composed on the road to large gulps of bad Madeira.

"Unplayable," he muttered. "Unplayable. There, that measure, impossible. Yet he does know the instrument. How do we handle these insane intervals? What is he up to?"

He picked up the guitar. He poised his fingers. "Unplayable, like everything he writes. Acrobatics . . . He cares only for acrobatics, not music."

He looked at his hands: short, sturdy, decent hands. Hands for honest work, not for the circus. He recalled one moment in the carriage, just before Milan. Paganini had become fired up and suddenly began to communicate Italian-style—a veritable dance of the fingers, a

ballet of gestures. Nicolo's hands were like two pale, flut-
tering birds tied to the end of a string.

*T*hey're back."

No need to go to the window and confirm it. The
admiring ladies had returned. A little time to change, put
on perfume, do their hair, and lower their necklines, and
they had come running back to settle in for the siege. The
official concert was not until the next day. But they would
not leave without an appetizer or a little tidbit exclusively
for them. They waited impatiently, they prowled about,
noisy and greedy. They could wait all night long. To them,
night was not meant for sleeping. Naps took care of that:
sleep and digestion from two to six, a time-saving device,
a way to revitalize for pleasure to come. Was anyone safe
from Italian women?

Amid all this theatrical hubbub, the approach of
something that rustled. Fabric, rather heavy, was brushing
the floor in the hallway. The rustling stopped. Luigi
smiled. It was not the first visit of the kind. Not all
women were seagulls. Some preferred rooms at the far

end of the hallway, accommodations made for the guitar.

"Don't get up for me. Keep playing."

The door had opened. With no fuss a fairy had sat down next to the musician. She was an aristocrat, as the gold ring with the little coronet indicated: "I have a right to be where I please, and tonight my pleasure is to be near you. Consider yourself fortunate and keep playing." All those unspoken words summed up in a little smile.

What could a musician do but give thanks to God, to music, to Italian countesses, and play? Play very low, as if telling a secret. Gradually the roar of the world faded away. He felt alone, favored, protected. The guitar knows how to create desert islands. . . .

I Cannone! Il Cannone!"

As usual, the master kept his audience waiting; the enthusiasts downstairs had grown impatient.

"Poor geese!" the countess exclaimed. "To prefer a violin . . . How should I put it? . . . to prefer a public violin to a guitar for one alone!"

Kneeling on the hearth, her head slightly bent, she

blew on the dying embers. Her back was bare, stylishly décolleté for evening. A teardrop earring dangled down her ever-so-long white neck and seemed to sway in time to the music. Black hair cascaded over her right shoulder. Luigi reached out to touch it.

"Please," said the lady. "There is no hurry. We have all the time in the world. And why deprive ourselves of the performance? Are you coming?"

She had stood up and was already opening the door. Luigi could not keep from making a face. "I'll join you. A few chords to go over."

*H*ere he is, at last. Nicolo Paganini appears. On the landing, all in white—ruffled shirt open, flowing trousers nipped in at the ankles Moorish style—he plays and, as is his custom, offers greetings in the nine languages he knows. He descends, one step at a time. He talks as he plays; he tells about himself. Intimate recollections, witticisms, juicy indiscretions. Seducing, always seducing, incorrigible Nicolo! Luigi does not have to strain: through the thin floor he hears all—the rest he guesses.

modest, almost timid. He is the grac

and he would be begging.

Upstairs, on the other

Luigi has gotten the mes

the bass strings are ne

ing Milan.

He stretch

dance. Imp

The fir

they

*N*ow Nicolo is bored. He has played all his tricks, taken all his poses, seduced all the women, and he is bored. Nothing worse than the boredom of the seducer. Opposite all those enamored faces, he feels alone in the world. A naked clown amid the crowd. Then he appeals, as instrumentalists appeal—by changing the game. He abandons his arrogance, forsakes his haughtiness, swears that he wishes to conquer no more, and he turns gentle,

...ious host. A little more

...side of the very thin ceiling,
...sage. He grabs his guitar. Luckily
...w. He changed them just before leav-

...es his fingers, smiles. And enters into the
...nediately his notes rise, powerful and warm.
...moldings amplify them, bounce them back, and
...resound as in a church.

The violin hesitates briefly. Its surprise can be felt: what, is it possible this little guitar has such mighty lungs? It is easy to guess the temptation: to take back the advantage at once, to crush as usual. But Nicolo has him on a short rein.

And music turns up again, the music that fled *Il Cannone*'s acrobatics in disgust. It returns a step at a time: it greets the fire in the hearth, it caresses the walls, it slides over the skin of the geese. With five or six measures, it takes away most of their silliness; a little more music, and the geese may get their souls back.

Guitar, violin, guitar, each plays its part; they respect each other, they listen to each other. Fragile equilibrium, a trifle can destroy it. Any duet is a duel. But Paganini has been so afraid, afraid of being alone. He has an overwhelming need for others. He is mastering his demons. For the moment.

*W*hen Clapton opened his eyes, the luminous watch dial said 4:00 A.M. Did African nights always involve such extensive traveling? He was worn out after changing countries, houses, and centuries so often, and after hurrying almost nonstop from Barcelona to Parma via golden, smelly Versailles. The guitar slept nestled against him, as usual. He glanced at it, frightened. He had just realized that witchcraft resided within that blond wooden box.

The camp was at rest. Completely calm and still. A light breeze barely ruffled the tent. It was the depths of night, the moment when even the seriously ill and the deeply distressed finally give in to sleep. But what was that sudden thump, soon followed by another? Why the beating in the darkness? Who would start drumming before dawn had plugged in its light-making equipment?

NANTES, GOREE ISLAND, MISSISSIPPI, 1800–1900

*N*antes, the fair city of Nantes . . ." On that particular night, Le Bozec hated Nantes. His hat dripping under the squall, he hurried along the quay, his destination the ship owners' quarter.

The summons had arrived on board at a late hour: "Lieutenant Le Bozec shall present himself . . ."

One had to obey orders. "Be apprised of the situation," as they put it, the masters of the Nantes trade. Heed all those overly polite phrases. And Le Bozec was furious.

The cabin boy had knocked and handed him the letter. ". . . shall present himself before the Company . . ."

A dinghy awaited him, floating alongside the ship.

"Nantes, the fair city of Nantes . . ." The nursery rhyme had entered his head unbidden, along with the anger. What one must do to earn a living . . . As a child, dreaming on the beaches of Saint-Malo, never would he have imagined such voyages. Might the sea herself sometimes feel shame?

The rain and the gusts hit against the windows and swept into the alleyways. Even inside the house, with shutters closed and drapes drawn, the flames flickered in the chandeliers.

"A schoolgirl excursion, my dear Le Bozec. Let the pilot off at Saint-Nazaire. To the port side, and head south. Straight south, and every sail set. Africa, young man . . . Pull at the ship. Always pull at the crew. Pull hard! The Company insists: rapid journeys . . . It wants the ship moving along like a dog running with a bone. Let the British see nothing but our behinds, Lieutenant . . ."

The ship owner put down his glass.

"The farewell glass of port!"

The fifth at least. Without port, who would depart? Wasn't Henry the Navigator Portuguese?

Le Bozec—polite—leaned over the map on the table. He followed a trembling finger. The signet ring and the peculiar hairs of the second digit swept across the Sahara and were gliding toward the Congo. The ship owner was lost; he hunted for the coast; he became impatient with the document. He could not find the blue. Or the secret destination of the voyage.

The wind was still rising, and Le Bozec thought about his ship. Lying at anchor, ready for the dawn sailing. At the turn of the tide. And each gust caused him pain: he pictured the hull, its planking, its ribs, bouncing in the choppy water, pulling on the two anchors. Holding firm, at best, or instead, dragging, drifting . . .

Sailor! Where is your pride, sailor?

And there was Le Bozec, bent over in a drawing room, cut in half, and deferential. Hat in hand dripping on the carpet. Having to follow a frail finger lost in the middle of the desert.

"Nantes . . ." The nursery rhyme materialized again. It filled his brain: "Fair city of Nantes." Hardly!

"Aha, here we are. Goree!" The ship owner put his index finger on a little island. Offshore, two miles from Dakar, Senegal.

Later Le Bozec thought, what will my children call me: sailor or slaver?

$\mathcal{L}$e Bozec would sail at dawn. Like so many others. His boat was named *La Vigilante*—two masts and a straight tiller.

At Goree, she would take on 227 men and 120 women. Iron collars for their necks. Arm irons and leg irons. Padlocks and keys. The two sexes well separated, a layer for each.

Anyone interested in the subject can look at the bills of lading in the Naval Museum: listed, what appears to be bags of stones for ballast. These are black people.

Goree, little island of tears off Dakar, concentration camp for slaves, last bit of African soil before the open sea, last beacon before the Americas.

*U*p to 1867, how many Le Bozecs?

How many little barefoot apprentices sculling, dreaming of being sailors? How many Le Bozecs trapped into living their lives in the infamous trade? And how many blacks would they transport, all these Le Bozecs? How many would they transport across the ocean, men and women in search of light and air, lying deep in the hold under the shiny deck of some *Vigilante*? Fifty million, one hundred million?

Goree Island. Shame of sailors!

*O*n countless occasions, seeing the blacks' distress, the guitar had wanted to offer its services. Wretched slaves, prisoners of cotton and sugar cane, shackled to their work. Wretched blacks of America, deprived of their music. The Black Code enforced by the planters was specific: the banning of drums and flutes, which "might be used as in Africa for communication and the call to rebellion." Capital punishment for offenders.

Those unfortunate souls had their vo
and work songs would echo from plant;

tion. And at church on Sundays they found signs of hope in the Bible, parallels. The Jewish people too had been in chains. And God had set them free. The slaves would sing until they were hoarse, would throw themselves into the words:

> *Go down, Moses, way down in Egypt's land*
> *Tell old Pharaoh, let my people go.*

It is good to sing together, to surrender the entire body to rhythm. But how alone the human voice feels when no instrument steps in to relieve it!

The banjo was permitted, and sometimes the fiddle. But how can sadness and exile be expressed with the dry and squeaky sounds of those instruments, caricatures of music, boxes lacking in subtlety, children's playthings?

The guitar remained as discreet as ever. It awaited its hour. It made ready in secret. Invisible, it walked all over the South; it hung around the cotton fields, the banks of the Mississippi, the swamps of the Delta. It even found a way into shanties and cabins, where it was attentive to sighs, entered dreams, sobbed to nightmares. It was learning the black soul and making the blues its own:

> The first time I met the blues,
>> he was walking through the woods.
> He knocked at my home
>> and done me all the harm he could.
> Now the blues got after me, Lord,
>> and run me from tree to tree.
> You should have heard me begging:
>> "Mister Blues, don't murder me."
> Good morning Mister Blues,
>> what are you doing here so soon?
> You be's with me in the morning
>> and every night and noon.*

Naturally, the guitar heartily applauded the end of slavery. But the guitar was not born yesterday. It is as old as the world. It knows that laws are often used to mask reality and that the good can engender the bad.

And the bad was there; the bad had seized the lands around the Mississippi and now ruled over them. The southerners were taking their revenge. The Ku Klux Klan and the Knights of the White Camellia pursued the form

---

* *Little Brother Montgomery.*

slaves. Lynchings became common. In 1883, more than eight hundred in one county alone. Segregation came in and reserved for the blacks the worst schools, the most insalubrious hospitals. And above all, lack of work. Manpower was no longer free; the old plantations struggled to survive, and people were laid off left and right. There was but one answer for blacks: the road. Escape to the North. Reach New York, Chicago, any of the big Yankee cities, where they might be able to find work.

*W*hen a man, after being uprooted from his continent, is driven from the land where his parents and the parents of his parents were born, only one homeland is left him: music.

ew breed sprang up to wander
1ey were given the name "song-
ongs, their ballads long tales of
society. They would knock at
tent cities, coffeeshops, restau-
for a meal and shelter for the
legends of Frankie and Albert,

Duncan and Brady, of Bill the railroad man, of the House of the Rising Sun . . .

Black religious sects increased and inhabited churches where believers would pray aloud and clap, as if trying to awaken God. And where they would call up from their common memory the old slave tunes, Negro spirituals that gradually turned into gospel songs. It was the preacher who directed the choir, it was he who stirred up the faithful.

The guitar had found its place, on the back of the songster, in the arms of the preacher. The black man sailed on his sorrow, and the guitar was his ship.

Their shared voyage became the blues.

PARIS, PORTE D'ITALIE, 1928

The big taxi glides along quietly in the dark. Under its long black hood, the eight-cylinder engine purrs, husky and muffled. It is the wee hours of the morning, when the dance halls close.

Barbès, Montmartre, Rue de Lappe . . . The driver is sleepy. He has made his rounds, tried his luck at the exit of every bar and club: the Ange Rouge and the Rose Blanche, even Gravilliers—the most dangerous when the lights go out. "Power failure," the owner will shout. "I'm closing my eyes!" And the pistols are cocked, the knives flash.

The streets are empty: a hard freeze tonight.

There's still the Java, a new place—music, poker, and a shady crowd. Last turn. Can't ever tell what luck will bring. A gift tonight perhaps, a peaceful drive in the same direction as home?

The driver lowers the window a little and wipes off the windshield. In front of the nightclub, blocking the street, a dark coupé has stopped, doors wide open. A pimp type—felt hat down, collar up, light overcoat—pulls along a young blonde in a beret and short dress. He throws her into the backseat and suddenly the car is lurching. A quick bit of love, with the engine running. The male is already on his feet; he gets out and slams the door. He shouts an address, somewhere in Montparnasse, hits the car with the flat of his hand, and goes back indoors to finish his port flip.

On the sidewalk, two fellows in caps are working over a third.

"Porte d'Italie. Head for the zone. I'll tell you where."

A man—very young—has entered the cab without a sound. Cigarette dangling from one corner of his mouth, he smiles and taps the black case he has tossed next to him on the worn velvet cushions.

"Empty," he says reassuringly.

The driver, surprised, turns around. This fare isn't even twenty. Where has he come from?

Slicked-down black hair gleaming in the light from the rear window. The narrow eyes are slanting. Like the high cheekbones and the mustache. A face made up of Vs, Vs in all directions.

Azerbaijan? Cherkassy? In any case, the features pure Asia.

The driver does not close the interior window: no separation tonight. Caution be damned! The need to talk is too strong.

He searches along the dashboard for the gearshift, the funny bayonet-shaped lever he must guide in its pattern.

While starting up, he introduces himself. He cannot bear his clientele being mistaken about him. "I am Russian, sir, noble house before the Revolution. Afteward, exile. Today, taxi. Such is life." He winks in the rearview mirror. A pleasant old gentleman, slight. How can such a voice come out of that small body? A true bass, a bourdon to rock a cathedral.

"I, sir, gypsy. Same story," replies the young man with the slicked-down hair. "Django. Profession, banjo . . ." He puts out his hand. "I'm Django, with Reinhardt, for the full name. . . . Or Jeangot Renard, as they say here."

"I am honored. Music, too, is a form of nobility." The driver has stopped to better greet his fare. He all but gets out on the sidewalk to stand at attention. He starts up again.

The aforementioned Django taps the black case. "Now it's my brother Joseph's turn. He's playing for me; we look alike. I leave him to work and I go home. The Java's lousy: twenty-seven pieces an hour for the *gadjé*. Bad music, but the money flows. . . . Besides, I'm done with the Java. A rich Englishman has just hired me."

"Congratulations."

"We'll see what happens."

On this frosty night, November 1, 1928, the Russian and his gypsy cross the Seine, go down the Boulevard de l'Hôpital, drive slowly by the Salpêtrière, reach the Italie neighborhood.

"Gypsy," repeats the driver. "In Russia, I came across a great many."

Just beyond the fortifications, Paris comes to a dead stop and the zone begins, that illegal city outside the city. Mud, standing water, garbage, wooden shacks, corrugated tin roofs, a little tavern about to collapse, a dead dog. Just a glance is enough to make one shudder. It's easy to imagine the army of rats, even in winter, and the pasty-faced children whose coughs last from October to March. Here and there a light. The rest languishes in darkness.

"Stop. Here we are. Treat yourself and thanks for the ride."

"You're sure?"

The Russian cabby has turned around. He holds the large bill in his hand. The empty case lies on the backseat. In the distance, a silhouette hurries between two remnants of the fortified wall and disappears. Who would dare go after him?

*O*n the other side of the slope, under the last quarter of the moon, the sleeping camp: a few multicolored jalopies and a hundred or so caravans in all sizes and shapes, some rich, some poor, some insane—a homemade assortment. And a little band of horse people poorly protected under the tin roofs.

Django stops, takes a deep breath: "They're going to be proud of me. . . ."

A few dogs have come out; they look at him but do not bark. Behind a red-curtained window, two silhouettes embrace. From two or three other interiors, the sounds of conjugal discussion as couples exchange pleasantries.

"Proud or not, who knows?"

The people here, brothers and cousins, think only of being on the road. Bella, though, will be overjoyed. Bella, who works all day to support them, crafting artificial flowers for graveside gardens.

He runs toward the wheeled house with his good news.

Bella awakens with a start. Django has leaped on the bed and is kissing her. She gropes in the dark and lights a candle. She is a woman who likes to look at happiness. Django, in his frenzy, knocks over everything. The candle falls on the celluloid flowers. And the caravan is on fire. Bella, her hair singed, manages to escape. She shouts, "Django's inside, Django's inside!"

He, overcome by smoke, crawls along the floor. The blaze surrounds him. In a last effort, he throws himself into the flames; somehow he gets through the burning curtain. He screams in pain, rolls on the ground. His whole body is a painful wound and his skin is already coming off in ribbons.

On this night of All Saints', 1928, a left hand enters into legend.

In spite of his injuries, or because of them, Django did not stay in the hospital long: they wanted to amputate his right leg. He flatly refused. His cousins came and took him back to the camp.

Months of torture followed.

"What are you thinking about?" his mother asked the invalid who lay shaking in his bed with fever.

"My hand."

His sores suppurated in spite of the daily sprinkling with various spices, the application of silver nitrate, and other sweet treatments. He had to return to the surgeons.

The left hand came back from the operating room nearly dead. The ring finger and the little finger were lost, inert forever, petrified, curled up against the palm like poor little useless claws. The rest of the hand was nothing but scars and scar tissue, reddish surfaces, folds . . . a kind of monster below the wrist. But Joseph, the musician brother, was well versed in legends. He knew that the only way to appease a monster was by offering him a beauty. One Sunday he did not come alone to the ward in the old Saint-Louis Hospital. He had brought along a big package, which he unwrapped slowly. Django shouted with delight. As of that day, the left hand suffered no longer. And all the white coats—doctors, nurses, physical therapists, technicians—and the chaplains came to observe, flabbergasted, the progress of the love affair between three fingers and a guitar.

"It can't be happening! That hand belongs to the devil!"

The index and middle fingers, sole survivors of the blaze, raced over the strings as if flames were still pursuing them: they slid, they plucked, they leaped, they fluttered, so pleased to be there again, and they harassed and jostled the guitar, made fun of its languor and modesty: come on, my girl, come on, my sister, stop groaning, we're made for delight! As for the thumb, no question of its staying put: it was determined to join the party. It would suddenly appear from behind the neck and peck the notes. As if it were the beak of a fighting cock or a bird gone mad.

The guitar simpered, took offense, like a countess played up to by some amorous punk at a black dance hall, and then she surrendered, gave in to a left hand so adept at whisking the soul away, offering it faraway landscapes, setting it down on a cloud. . . .

$\mathcal{L}$ater, the jazz greats—Duke Ellington, Coleman Hawkins—went wild over that left hand. Forgetting all else, and whatever the price, they wanted it in their orchestras. The left hand would always promise but did not show up very often. Looking for it meant going from bar to bar, all night sometimes.

Genuine left hands are like that. They have cut all ties with the constraints of daily life.

WOODSTOCK, 1969

*R*ain.

Rain always had the same magical effect on him. As soon as the first drops fell, as soon as dampness and the faint smell of earth rose from the ground, a door would open in his skull. And the memories would rush in.

Yes, rain was allied with memory, for better or for worse.

And God knows it rained on America, that August!

Huddled in the meadow, the crowd protected itself as best it could. As far as the eye could see, blankets quivered in the night, plastic covers glistened under the flashes of lightning, hats flew in the wind. The crowd was waiting. Waiting for the concert to resume. Waiting and sinking into the mud. A tepid mud, which, once the body's initial revulsion was past, shaped itself perfectly to the contours of the buttocks, gently caressed the legs, and fit—warm and friendly—between the thighs.

Inside his car, jammed between Mitch and Billy, Jimi was smoking, windows open wide in spite of the deluge.

An organizer took the mike: "If we all want it very much, the rain will stop. Do we want it?"

"We want it!" shouted the crowd.

But the rain continued. The rain was like life, stubborn and cruel and sweet, as indifferent as life. Eventually the rain was going to dissolve the crowd. All the nice young people, wet and weary, would go back home. Finished, the great concert, drowned. Missed, the rendezvous. And Jimi would be alone. Just as when his life began, just as when his mother died.

$\mathcal{D}$addy, what color is my skin?"

I am eleven. I live in a ghetto overwhelmed by interchanges. What color is the skin of a motherless child deafened by freeways?

VERTIGO BOOKS
7346 Baltimore Ave.   301-779-9300

319592   Reg 1 12:12 pm 08/14/07

S HIST OF THE WORLD   1 @   4.99   4.99
SUBTOTAL   4.99
TAX   .25
TOTAL   5.24
VISA PAYMENT   5.24
Account# 4294046061001970   Exp 1107
Authorization# 014156

I agree to pay the above total amount
according to the card issuer agreement.

Returns for store credit/exchange only

My father's name is James. He is a gardener. He doesn't talk much. But when you ask him a question, he knows how to answer: "Sorry, son. You are red and black. Because of me being black. Because of your mother being a Cherokee Indian. In this country, it isn't the easiest skin to carry around. Sorry, you'll have to make do."

I have restless fingers. They won't stay still. They tap on every surface they see. They beat time on the walls and the tables, on my desk at school. They live their own life, and I can't do anything about it. It's no good telling them to stop. They don't hear me. They like handles better than anything: the ones on my father's tools, his mattocks, spades, and brooms.

My father doesn't just know how to answer. He knows how to look: "I've seen your fingers, son. They'll end up hurting you. The world is tough, tougher than fingertips. Yours are waiting for something, you can depend on it. All the fidgeting, that's their way of calling. Now I've brought you something. Do you think maybe it's what they've been waiting for?"

I am eleven. My father has just taken the guitar from behind his back. A big brown box with strings. My fingers are happy. They have found their garden, their house, their promenade, a door to the world, a way to speak. They know that my Cherokee mother will hear me this time, in spite of her death, in spite of the noise from the interchanges.

The gardener nods. He follows the fingers frolicking on the guitar and nods. He has the manners of the shy: only someone who knows him would read the contentment under the dark mask. "Good, son. When your skin's the wrong color, you need fingers that dance. Fingers that dance make music. And in music, the color of your skin doesn't matter."

The father goes to the table and takes two spoons from the drawer. The spoons are his percussion section; hitting them together he can produce any beat. The interchanges are silent; they realize that a major event is underway on the Pacific Coast, here in Seattle, Washington.

Interchanges are no more stupid nor evil than anything else. If they make such a racket, if they roar so loud, it is for a simple reason: the ghetto air is empty, the ghetto air has nothing to say. But for once, these interchanges open their ears. The father hums a theme. The son's fingers discover it, flush it out note by note in the forest of the strings. The father's happiness grows. His son has that most intelligent of ears, the ear that knows how to give fingers the right orders. The wandering soul of the guitar has just chosen its new home: a red and black child. Let his parents look on, dumbfounded: a living gardener, who is torturing his spoons, and a dead Cherokee mother, who is quietly applauding. The interchanges are silent.

*R*ain was still falling, finer now in the night, more gentle, the downpour replaced by drizzle. The crowd was leaving. It could no longer endure the water, the mud, nor the silence that had followed three days of wild music. The empty stage and the speaker-covered towers rose in the dark like the ruins of an abandoned fortress.

The crowd felt afraid and was leaving amid the muck, babies on backs and fiancées helped along; it was in retreat, in long dark lines that flowed like water.

I'll be alone again, Jimi said to himself, huddled in his car. Alone, as before.

And while the rain, that damned courier of memories, went on falling, he relived his beginnings: the terrible sixties, those lean and hungry times, dreary days and sordid nights, the five-dollar motels, the hitchhiking, the shabby stages, the audiences that booed or walked out (just like tonight), the managers who would disappear on payday, the partners who changed all the time, the partners who stole from you, the jealous partners who would kindly offer you a glass of water right before your entrance, water full of cocaine or poison or acid, and you'd go crazy out there on the stage. . . .

Wretched music! It had not come on its own. It had to be conquered, note by note, chord after chord. Most likely, his music came from misery. Misery that entered through the skin, through the eyes. That invaded Jimi's skull. And then, under the hair and the bone, mystery, metamorphosis. The fingers moved up and down the neck of the guitar. Misery had turned into music. Misery, skin, head, fingers, guitar, music: A hundred times Jimi went that same cursed, magical route, along a path that would start out so badly and end up creating such happiness. Music was the daughter of misery. Music was misery's song. He remembered the rotten evening that had given him the melody for "Stone Free," and the dreadful trip that had inspired "Highway Chile."

Yeah! His guitar is strung across his back,
His dusty boots is his Cadillac.
I'm flamin' here, just blowin' in the wind,
Ain't seen a bed I'm so long a misdecent.
He left home when he was seventeen,
The rest of the world he is gonna see.
And ev'rybody they know his boss,
A rolling stone,
To gather its own moss.
Have you probably
Called him a tramp?
But it goes a little deeper than that,
He is a . . . highway chile.
Yeah!

$\mathcal{L}$ost in his dreams, lulled by his memories, Jimi had not seen the night fade, had not noticed the faint light of dawn settling in the black sky. He had not heard the festival awakening for the last time, nor caught the smell of hot coffee, nor attended to the sounds that once again issued from the tall speaker towers. It cannot be denied that the group scheduled for this Monday morning was particularly dismal. Sha Na Na: a band of idiots, a cross between cosmonauts in gold suits and loutish sailors in striped jerseys, a show for the off-season at a casino.

A tap on the shoulder.

"It's time."

Words for a man about to be executed.

"It's all yours."

"Mine?"

"Yes, yours to end."

"End?"

"End. End the three days. End the greatest concert in the world, and forever. All yours, Jimi!"

And Jimi stood up. There he was, on stage.

Before him, as far as the eye could see, what had been a field, a green midsummer meadow, was now nothing but mud. And very close, at his feet, surrounding him, encircling him, clasping him like so many arms, were three thousand lunatics, still there in spite of the wind and the rain, in spite of their overwhelming desire to sleep, three thousand stalwarts determined to hear Jimi do battle with music.

His friends stepped back—Mitch (Mitchell) and Billy

(Cox). Juma Edwards, the drummer, ill at ease, looked like a timid little boy. The Ghetto Fighters, tough guys though they were, did not dare step forward. They waited. Like everyone else. They were waiting for the duel.

Jimi was alone. At twenty-seven, with thirteen months left to live. He stepped forward, wrapped in his legend, dressed in his grandiose funky finery. A raspberry headband. Mother-of-pearl button earrings. Gold chain and opal locket. White leather jacket with long fringes against bare skin. Jeans held up by a belt of emerald beads. The weapon was ivory, a masterpiece by Leo Fender, a stratocaster with a long neck of pale wood. A wide multicolored strap—red, yellow, black, white—fastened it to Jimi's neck.

"The Star Spangled Banner." Unable to believe it, the crowd heard the first notes of the National Anthem. People looked at each other. What insanity was in the offing? Jimi was capable of anything. But attacking the symbol of the United States? What could a guitar accomplish against the world's number one power?

Fearless, the stratocaster mounted the assault, taking the anthem out of itself, bending it, twisting it, wringing it. Suddenly, the melody seemed to be asking for mercy. But

Jimi was pitiless. He had come to Woodstock with his faint smile to force, to break, to shatter the starry banner. He wanted to show what was backstage, in the wings: the horrors behind the noble, peaceful facade. He would not let the anthem go; he pressed it, he threatened it, and the anthem finally broke down and confessed. Confessed to the bombing of Vietnam, the napalming of villages. Jimi's ringed fingers could not keep up with the confession. His fingers pleaded: slower, softer! We cannot handle it all! But the floodgates had opened, the admissions poured out. Pushed to the limit, America had stopped pretending. She caterwauled, she howled.

Jimi struck his strato. One day he would rip it open, thanks to his heavy-handedness with the vibrato controls. Another time, he would even bite it. Yes, because of finding his fingers too soft, he was to play with his teeth.

Never before had the guitar expressed the madness of the world in such a way; nor would it do ever do so again. Who says that music is sweet? Tentative, barely on its feet, the melody was led astray, tortured, trampled.

Mitch and Billy left him alone in his duel to the death. Juma Edwards watched the struggle, fascinated and terrified, as he leaned against his drums.

Jimi stopped.

The world was nothing but smoking ruins. On the ground, the American flag twitched and sputtered, hard hit. Woodstock was silent a moment, holding its breath. The only sounds were the chirping of birds, the squealing of children. It was the silence of humans after battle, the silence in which to gather up the dead. Jimi was still alive. Not for long. Battling adversaries stronger than oneself leaves wounds that do not heal. Unseen hemorrhages deep inside, red lakes that spread out and lead to drowning. The bravos that mounted had no power against them, nor did the enthusiasm.

Thirteen months later he died in London, the knight with the multicolored funky finery and the sad black and red face, the Don Quixote of the guitar.

OMO VALLEY (AFRICA), 31 DECEMBER 1999

$\mathcal{E}$asy, easy . . ."

Clapton was struggling. Crouched on the sleeping bag, he waved his arms in all directions. His temples glistened with sweat. Eyelids screwed up and brow wrinkled, mouth open, he seemed to be passing through a long airless tunnel. Bent over him in the tiny tent, the old archaeologist had a hand on each shoulder and was trying to calm him down. He spoke as one would to a runaway horse: "Easy, easy, you're alive, it's dawn, it's going to be a beautiful day."

Clapton slowly opened his eyes. He was shaking. He spoke in gasps, as if each syllable were another step on an endless staircase.

"This time, I really thought I'd never come back."

"Come back?"

"Come back from the night."

"You shouted several times: 'Thank you, thank you, Jimi!'"

"I was with him."

"Is this Jimi someone who lives far away?"

"Much too far, even for someone like me who enjoys traveling."

Clapton was beginning to feel like himself again. The old archaeologist slipped outside. The air was cool and smelled of hot coffee.

"Look, I think we have company."

Clapton came out too and stretched luxuriously. Never had he looked so tall. He ran his hands back and forth through his damp hair and dried and redried his glasses on his shirt.

To the north, a man and a horse were coming along the river road from the old capital, Addis, where it was unwise to stroll alone and unarmed, where war continued for reasons unknown to all, but perhaps simply as a way to avoid boredom and inhale once again the warm odor of blood in the sand. The horse proceeded at a walk. The man appeared exhausted. Every so often he would rest his upper body against the animal's neck. Then, with a terrible effort of the will, he would sit up straight again. From the knees down, under the black overcoat, he wore white hose that ended in patent leather pumps.

"What a costume for Africa!"

"I recognize him," said Clapton. "I'm going to greet him."

The shepherds did not move. They were huddled around the fire, wrapped in their cloaks. Why had the traveler become frightened? He was shaking all over. He shouted: "My name is Joan Carlos Amat. I cured Barcelona, I am the doctor of boredom. . . . My name is Doctor Amat."

After a few minutes of this pathetic sight (a white man with powdered hair, frozen and terrified), a woman, overcome by pity, left the group to go stroke the doctor's knee. She had that eagerness of mouth, eyes, body, and hands not unusual among women of the region. Gradually the man from Barcelona became less agitated. He dismounted and sat down. They offered him a bowl of milk. One of the shepherds pointed to the horizon and mimed a man walking: "Where do you come from?"

Amat took a little sand and let it run through his fingers.

The shepherd understood: this traveler came from inside time.

*N*ot long after, two white vehicles appeared from behind the hill, bouncing, jumping over the ruts, half disappearing into the giant holes. A closer look revealed that one was pulling the other. And those among the shepherds who had some experience with civilization recognized a German car—an old Mercedes—and a six-wheeled caravan of undetermined age and nationality.

These travelers had none of the shyness of the earlier arrival. As soon as their convoy stopped, a dozen stocky fellows with dark curly hair leaped out, brandishing their guitars like scimitars.

"Wake up, Django," they shouted, "we're here."

The night, terrified by the din, had departed without further ado.

Thousands of flamingoes, perched on one leg, flapped their wings. Smaller birds fluttered around them like attentive valets. A few patches of light fog still clung to the reeds along the shore. But these cottony traces would not linger, for the bright African day was soon to extend its benevolent empire over all things.

*I*t was like the first day of school after summer vacation. One by one, guitarists arrived from every country and every era. The veterans were joined by an endless stream of newcomers (Corbetta, his court costume all beribboned; Paganini, with the lost look of the star not yet sure which camera is filming him; two songsters from Louisiana, received like kings by the shepherds—at last, some blacks!—and fussed over by their giant wives; a lady from Seville with a bald husband and a red dress, angry at not finding African soil hard enough for flamenco; three Brazilians, adopted sons of Baden-Powell, whispering until nightfall bossa novas as sweet as almond milk).

Introductions, handshakes, memories: music is the ally of beginnings, as is darkness when shy lovers come together the first time. No need for words, or gestures, or even smiles. One note, one chord is enough; another answers, everything takes shape, everything intertwines: it is done.

After their momentary astonishment (were they really guitars, these big multicolored beans bristling with knobs and switches?), they traded instruments, they learned each other's secrets.

Doctor Amat would not let go of his Gibson Firebird. Coy as a virgin, he was discovering what electricity could do, the power of a speaker, the muffled thunder of stacks. A gaunt Peruvian, an early afternoon arrival, had abandoned his *charango* for a stratocaster. At each note produced he would jump, as if each time he were stepping on a dragon's tail.

Sitting in a corner on a crate addressed to the Musée de l'Homme, Place du Trocadéro, 75016, Paris, and marked FRAGILE, Clapton was teaching a Stradivarius the blues. He spoke softly of the Mississippi. Under his fingers, the instrument turned sultry. A young gypsy, Django's nephew, had gotten hold of a treasure from the seventeenth century; away from the mocking gaze of his family, he stroked its mother-of-pearl inlay and fine rosewood marquetry with his oil-stained fingernails.

The scientists, specialists in early humans, had put aside their toothbrushes. They sat in their tomblike pits and took in all the scattered strains of music, a concert meriting the envy of the lake birds. The director of the dig, the old archaeologist, looked on with a broad smile; ever since the night before, he had been thoroughly enjoying himself. He put a hand on Clapton's shoulder: "Hurrah for your previous lives! They are all very likable. Are you expecting more company?"

At first, no more than a rustle somewhere near the horizon. Gradually changing to a rumble. Ending as thunder, while the dust rose toward the sky in columns only to fall again in thick clouds that inundated everything.

The pink helicopter flew over the lake, taunted the flamingoes, searched in vain for crocodiles, and finally landed.

"Terribly sorry we're late," exclaimed George Harrison, the first to step out, bending low to avoid the blades. "But we had to take a roundabout route. Someone very dear had left us, and he was living far away."

Paul and Ringo were seen next, and a few seconds later, John Lennon, more Asiatic than ever, with his crewneck tunic and the little round glasses of a mischievous mandarin. It was he who dwelt far away, the one the three others had spent such a long time finding.

They seemed delighted to be a foursome again. Their hair had turned white. That was the only sign of their years. In everything else, they were still twenty. They pounded one another on the back, adolescents once more, thanks to the pink helicopter.

And like insolent adolescents, they began to play with no thought for the others. Gaiety does not ask itself who should go first; it takes its guitar and plays.

And so, once again "Lucy in the Sky" rose in the African sky as night was falling. "Lucy in the Sky with Diamonds."

Flabbergasted at first, disgruntled ("We didn't come all this way just to have to listen to some old British tune"), the guitarists of other centuries entered into the dance one by one, conquered by the joie de vivre of the white-haired quartet.

The first to join in was Doctor Amat, known for his devotion to the art of happiness. He rose and continued the little Liverpool melody from where he stood.

Welcome, said John and Paul's sweeping gestures, welcome to Lucy's home; you who have set the example, who is going to follow you? They were using a minimum of electricity, playing as softly as possible—pretty respectful for punks. No question of a battle of the decibels on this night!

The doctor had finished his section and sat down. Django took over. A wave of the hand, hello, my old comrades! Lucy had taken to the road, Lucy was leaving Africa for Central Europe, Lucy was telling Gypsy tales. . . .

The scientists had drawn closer. The music had brought them out of their holes so rich in ancestral fragments. And while Corbetta played and then Django, they danced from one foot to the other: "Lucy, do you remember 1978, when we discovered the famous fifty-two bones? . . . I wasn't here, but they told me about it. . . . The first real woman in the history of the world . . ."

The old archaeologist went up to Clapton: "You certainly have a gift for celebrations. Only Hendrix is missing. He isn't the type to pay attention to schedules, maybe?"

"Hendrix will not be coming. He has gone too far. No one will ever be able to bring him back." His voice was hoarse.

"I'm sorry," said the old archaeologist.

"The inconsolable is part of life."

*C*ome on, Eric, come with us." The quartet was calling him. "Come on, quick, all this time we've been want-
ing to play with you."

First Clapton greeted Lucy, paying her homage with
four or five notes, a few bars, "in the Sky with Diamonds"—the sort of thing he did so well. Then his fingers,
which could convey any emotion no matter how fragile or
fleeting or vague, just as a painter can convey clouds, his
fingers went back to childhood and the well-known tune
that goes with turning off the light and bringing out a
cake: "Happy Birthday," at first very low, for him alone,
then taken up by his neighbors Harrison and Lennon.

"Happy Birthday, Lucy!"

Night had fallen over Africa, the twinkling African
night, spangled with stars: the three million candles on
Lucy's cake. Impossible to count. Besides, more and more
lights, little flames, were coming out on the hill around the
camp. The friends of the guitar had finally reached the
concert site. In spite of their long, very long trip, they still
had the strength to wave their cigarette lighters in time to
the music.

The scientists sang like the others. But they could not

help thinking about the beginnings of the world—their obsession . . .

Once drought had stripped the forest bare, Lucy stood up and watched for enemies. She felt naked and alone on her hind legs in the bare forest. That is when the need arose in her for something to hold, something to keep her company and speak to a world stripped bare. A hundred thousand years went by, perhaps, between Lucy's solitude, her need for music, and the making of the first guitar, a gourd strung with catgut . . . Or perhaps a hundred and ten thousand.

Lucy was joyful. She had waited a long time for her party, but what is time to the first woman in the world? She did not blow out her three million candles until dawn. The guitar players had disappeared. That did not surprise her. She knew the curse hanging over our species: the more humans there are, the greater their solitude.